Contents

Ladybird books are widely available, but in case of
difficulty may be ordered by post or telephone from:

Ladybird Books – Cash Sales Department
Littlegate Road Paignton Devon TQ3 3BE
Telephone 01803 554761

A catalogue record for this book is available
from the British Library

Published by Ladybird Books Ltd Loughborough Leicestershire UK
Ladybird Books Inc Auburn Maine 04210 USA

farmyard
stories for
under fives

by JOAN STIMSON

illustrated by
REBECCA ARCHER

Ladybird

Philippa's ride

"OUCH!" squealed Philippa Piglet. "I've cut my trotter."

"Never mind," said Mum briskly. She began to lick it better.

But, when Farmer Fred saw the cut, he was worried. So he drove Philippa to the vet.

At bedtime Philippa's brothers admired the bandage. But Philippa simply stared into the distance. "It was WONDERFUL!" she sighed.

"What was?" chorused her brothers.

"My ride in Farmer Fred's landrover," whispered Philippa and promptly fell asleep.

From then on all Philippa could think about was travel.

But Philippa's trotter had healed now. There was no need to visit the vet again. So, whenever Farmer Fred found her by the landrover, he always said the same thing. "Come on, let's put you back where you belong."

And with that he would tuck Philippa under his arm and carry her back to her family.

"Never mind," said Mum briskly, when it happened again. She pushed an apple towards Philippa.

But Philippa DID mind and she was busy making a plan.

Early next morning the little piglet squeezed through the gate that led to the lane. Just along the lane was a bus stop. Philippa had been watching it from the farmyard.

"If I wait here long enough," she told herself, "I can have another ride!"

"Whatever next!" cried a man weighed down with parcels. He had staggered off the bus and had almost fallen over Philippa.

The bus driver jumped off, too.

"Come on," he said to Philippa. "Let's put you back where you belong." The bus driver took Philippa back to the farmyard.

"Never mind," said Mum briskly. "I've saved you an acorn."

But Philippa DID mind, because more than anything else, she still wanted to travel.

Later that morning Farmer Fred had a visitor. He arrived with a squeal of tyres in a red sports car. Philippa arrived with a squeal of excitement. As soon as the visitor was out of sight, she began to investigate.

"TOOOOOOOT!"

"Who's sounding my horn?" boomed a voice from the farmhouse door.

The visitor strode across the yard. But Philippa had already disappeared into the nearest barn where Farmer Fred's son was polishing his motorbike.

"Hello!" he chuckled. "Would you like a spin… back to where you belong?"

Philippa rushed forward eagerly. But then she froze in her tracks because Mum was standing in the doorway… looking stern!

"PHILIPPA!" she cried. "Big motorbikes are too fast and too noisy for small piglets!"

Philippa sulked all evening. She slept badly all night and woke late and grumpy next morning.

"DING-A-LING-LING! ANYONE COMING FOR A RIDE?"

It was Farmer Fred's daughter on her new bike. And behind the bike was a little trailer.

Mum nudged Philippa forward. "Go on," she said briskly.

"HOORAY!" cried Farmer Fred's daughter. She lifted Philippa up. "All the other animals ran away. But you look as if you BELONG in my trailer."

Round and round the farmyard rode the little girl and the little piglet.

They both squealed as loudly as each other. And, however hard you looked, it was quite impossible to tell which of them enjoyed it most!

The ghost of Farthing Farm

"Isn't it DARK?" whispered Joel. He was staying with Mike at Farthing Farm. Joel came from the town.

"Isn't it QUIET?" he whispered a few minutes later. Joel was used to street lights and traffic.

At last Mike and Joel settled down. But not for long.

"Whatever's THAT?" cried Joel. He sat up in bed and shivered. "It sounds like a ghost," he whispered, "a very unhappy ghost!"

Mike rubbed his eyes and groaned. "It's just one of the sheep bleating," he explained patiently.

Joel settled down again. But in no time at all he was digging Mike in the ribs.

"Whatever's THAT?" he cried. "It sounds like a ghost… a ghost with dreadful tummy-ache!"

"It's just one of the cows mooing," explained Mike, a little less patiently.

Joel crept out of bed and peered through the window. He thought he could see some sheep and cow shapes. Joel began to feel better.

But suddenly Mike was clutching at JOEL'S pyjamas. "Whatever's THAT?" he shrieked.

Joel smiled sleepily. "It must be one of your animals," he said.

"But it's NOT!" cried Mike. "I know all the animal noises and I've NEVER heard anything like that."

Both boys peered out gingerly. The moon came out from behind a cloud.

"HELP!" cried Mike and Joel together.

In the field opposite was a ghostly figure. It had a huge pale head, which swayed and MOANED in the moonlight.

All of a sudden Mum appeared outside in her dressing gown. She seemed to wrestle with the figure. And then Mike burst out laughing.

"It's Ned, our donkey!" he cried.

When Mum came back inside, she was carrying an empty potato sack.

"No wonder poor Ned was making such a strange noise," she said. "He'd been looking for scraps and got his head stuck."

Mum tucked in the boys again and smiled.

"Whoever said it's always quiet in the country?" she asked.

"Not me!" whispered Joel and fell fast asleep until morning.

Chickens

We are the chickens,
(In case you hadn't guessed!)
We are the chickens,
We think you'll be impressed!

We slide down the haystack,
We balance on the coop,
We fly in strict formation
And ALWAYS loop the loop!

We dive from the dovecot,
We stagger to a stop,
We like to chase the sheep
And then to ride on top!

We bounce on the tractor,
We give the horn a BEEP,
We gallop round the yard
And NEVER go to sleep!

We are the chickens!
Our farmer needs a rest,
But still he tells his friends,
"MY CHICKENS ARE THE BEST!"

Gus goes to playgroup

"I don't want to go to playgroup," said Jenny, "…not unless Gus comes."

Jenny lived on a farm and Gus was a new goat.

"Jenny," sighed Dad, "I've already explained. Playgroup is for children, not for animals."

"But it's my first day," complained Jenny. "I won't know anybody."

Dad rang up Mrs Wright, the playgroup leader, for advice.

Playgroup had already started. You could tell by the din. But Mrs Wright shouted cheerfully down the line, "That will be fine. You'd be surprised what some children bring... particularly on their first day!"

Dad, Jenny and Gus all set off for playgroup. When they arrived, Mrs Wright was ticking names on a list.

"Trevor," she smiled, "THAT'S a nice train. Paul," she went on, "I DO like your panda. And YOU must be Jenny," beamed Mrs Wright.

Then she saw Gus.

"Good heavens!" cried Mrs Wright, turning to Dad. "I thought you said Jenny was bringing a BOAT. But now I see, it's a GOAT!"

Dad began to apologise, but Mrs Wright shooed him away. "Gus can stay for today," she said.

As soon as Dad left, Gus began to explore. One of the new children began to cry. And in no time at all, half the playgroup was crying.

Suddenly the tears turned to laughter. "WHEEEE!" Gus had squeezed himself into the playgroup pushchair and was whizzing across the floor.

"Thank goodness!" cried Mrs Wright. She settled the children to play.

Jenny began a painting. But Gus wanted to help. Jenny's picture didn't turn out as she planned.

Halfway through the morning the children had a snack.

"My word!" cried Mrs Wright. "I've NEVER seen such MESSY eaters!"

Suddenly Gus swept along like a hoover. Crumbs, crisps, apple cores, banana skins… it was all the same to Gus.

"Well done, Gus!" cried Mrs Wright. She began organising the children again.

Jenny wanted to try the slide. But so did Gus.

"HELP!" cried Jenny. "We're stuck!"

Mrs Wright untangled Jenny and Gus. But another tangle had started… by the clay. Paul and Susie were fighting.

"WHEEEE, PLOP!" Susie threw Paul's panda right on top of the cupboard.

"Oh no!" cried Mrs Wright. She HATED ladders.

But, before she could fetch one, Gus leaped to the rescue. He wanted to practise his climbing and SOARED from the top of the slide… right onto the cupboard. Then he bounced back down again. And panda bounced down, too!

"What a relief," said Mrs Wright. She looked at her watch and lined up the chairs for storytime.

Jenny wanted to sit next to Susie. But Gus pushed in first, just as Dad arrived.

"I do hope Gus hasn't been a nuisance," he began.

Mrs Wright shook her head and beamed. But, before she could say anything, Jenny piped up, "Yes, he has, Dad. And tomorrow I want to paint and go down the slide and make new friends ON MY OWN!"

So Gus didn't go to playgroup again. But, later that year, Jenny invited her new friends to the farm.

The playgroup children loved meeting the animals. But most of all they enjoyed seeing Gus again.

"Hasn't he grown!" they cried.

"Yes, he has," said Mrs Wright. She watched Gus charge round the farmyard. "And, although Gus is a WONDERFUL goat, he is definitely… TOO BIG FOR PLAYGROUP!"

The sheep who liked to be different

Scruff liked to be different. If the rest of the flock sat down for a chat and a chew, then Scruff went for a jog. If the other sheep started a stampede, Scruff simply turned her back and munched quietly in a corner.

She gave the sheepdog a terrible time. Whenever he got the sheep running one way, Scruff changed direction and sent them all scattering.

"I've never known a sheep with such a mind of her own!" said Farmer Field.

One warm, sunny day an interesting piece of news reached the flock. It was time for their first shearing. And the shearer was coming the next day.

This news set the sheep bleating. Some of them didn't want to be shorn.

"We'll look DAAAAAAFT!" they complained.

Others were all for it. "This weather is too hot!" they cried. "We want to feel cool!"

But on one thing the sheep were generally agreed. If Farmer Field had decided to shear them, then shorn they would be.

Scruff, of course, had other ideas. She was proud of her thick, curly coat and had no intention of losing it.

Early next morning Scruff set off… to find a hiding place. After a time she came to an old toolshed. The door was half-open. So, with a quick glance over her shoulder, she nipped inside.

"Perfect!" she announced and settled down under the workbench for a snooze.

By lunchtime the shearer was well on with his work. Farmer Field had his hands full helping and in the excitement NO ONE missed Scruff.

It was another blazing hot day. Very soon cheerful cries of "THAAAT'S MUUUUCH BEEEEETTER!" could be heard all over the fields.

But Scruff felt worse! The bleating had woken her up and given her a headache. She was beginning to feel hungry and to make matters even worse, the sun was beating down directly onto the toolshed roof.

"I'm too hot!" decided Scruff. She made for the toolshed door. But a rare gust of wind had blown it shut. Scruff was a prisoner!

She clambered onto the workbench and looked miserably through the window. In the distance she could see all her friends.

"If only I could be shorn!" sighed Scruff.

"Rattle, rattle, click!" Scruff jumped down eagerly from the bench. Someone was at the shed door.

It was Mrs Field, the farmer's wife. She didn't see Scruff for dust.

"ZOOOOM!" Scruff shot out of the shed and POUNDED across the field.

The shearer was just packing up his equipment.

"I might have guessed!" said Farmer Field.

The sheepdog sniffed in disgust.

"I'm sorry," said the shearer. "My blade's blunt. And it's my last one. I don't see HOW I can make this sheep look like the rest."

Farmer Field turned to the shearer and grinned.

"Now, don't you worry about THAT," he said. "Scruff LIKES to be different."

So, in the end, Scruff had the best of both worlds. She was soon cool and comfortable again. But, because the shearer's blade was blunt, Scruff was given a style… ALL OF HER OWN!

The chewalong song

CHEW, CHEW,
I DO love a CHEW!
There's nothing like breakfast
All covered in dew.
There's no need to buy it,
Or even to fry it,
So why don't you try it
And CHEW!

MUNCH, MUNCH,
I DO love a MUNCH!
There's nothing like clover
For flavouring lunch.
Although it grows thickly
You won't find it sickly,
So gather some quickly
And MUNCH!

GRAZE, GRAZE,
I DO love a GRAZE!
There's nothing quite like it
On warm, sunny days.
So please share my dinner,
This field is a winner!
We'll never grow thinner,
Let's GRAZE!

Too busy to hiss

"Ready!" cried Mother Goose. The goslings stood tall.

"Steady!" she yelled. The goslings leaned forwards.

"GO!" thundered Mum. And the goslings all HISSED… all except Henry.

"Sorry, Mum," said Henry. "I'm too busy to hiss. I'm meeting my friend the lamb. She's teaching me to jump."

"HENRY!" called Mum after him. "Just be on time for your NEXT lesson."

But Henry was LATE for his next lesson. And, when he got there, he couldn't concentrate.

"HISSSSSS!" went Henry's brothers.

"One, two, three, four, five, seven, ten," mumbled Henry. He watched the ducklings carefully as they waddled past.

"HENRY!" cried Mum. "What DO you think you're doing?"

"Sorry, Mum," said Henry. "I'm too busy to hiss. I'm learning to count."

The next day Henry's brothers hissed their hearts out. But Henry just stood to one side and stared. Then he caught Mum's eye.

"Sorry, Mum," said Henry. "I'm too busy to hiss. I'm admiring the view."

"HENRY!" bellowed Mum. "Go and admire the view somewhere else. I am VERY cross."

Henry didn't like the look in Mum's eye. He scuttled off so fast that he bumped bang into some bales of straw.

Henry picked himself up. But something was wrong. He could just see a thin curl of smoke. It was coming from the straw!

"HELP!" thought Henry. "It's a fire!"

Henry didn't hesitate. He jumped high into the air and gave the loudest HISSSSSSSSSS ever!

Lambs came bleating. Ducks came quacking. Mum came beaming. And the farmer came running. They ALL wanted to know WHAT had made Henry hiss.